£6.99

Published by Alligator Books Ltd
Gadd House, Arcadia Avenue
London N3 2JU
Printed in China

NICKELODEON

Rugrats

Contents

Meet the Rugrats

Angelica

This three-year-old tyrant puts the me in "me me me!" Angelica Pickles is a spoilt bully who always needs to be the centre of everyone's attention. When the other Rugrats see her coming to play — they dive for cover! The worst of it is that the grown ups think she's as angelic as her name because when she sees an adult around, she's as nice as pie.

Kimi

Always looking on the bright side, Kimi is open-hearted and full of fun! But whereas Chuckie is scared of everything, Kimi is scared of nothing and is always the first baby in the gang to boldly go where no baby has ever gone before! It's a bit daunting for Chuckie though who wants to look after his brand new little sister but is super scared of practically everything!

Dil

Dil, like most babies, seems to cry all the time. In fact when the Rugrats first met him they thought he was broken! Even though he cries a lot, Tommy loves his little brother very much and feels that it's his "sponsibility" to teach him all about the world. Even though his tantrums are hair-raising, he gets away with it every time, as he is irresistibly cute!

Chuckie

This two-year-old sees monsters in every wardrobe and creepy goblins in every dark corner! When the Rugrats start out on a new adventure he's always the first to point out the hundreds of things that could go wrong. However, being Tommy's best friend and Kimi's big brother he always follows along, even though he might complain the whole way!

Susie

Because of her energy, happy outlook and helpful advice, all the Rugrats babies look up to Susie. Susie always stands up for what's right, which often puts her directly in the path between Angelica and the Rugrats! Using the kind of wisdom that only comes with experience — she is three after all — she tries her best to solve all the problems and keep everyone happy.

Phil & Lil

Next door to Tommy and Dil live the DeVille twins, Phil and Lil. Mud pies, worms and "prettyful" bugs are some of these terrible twosome's favourite things. They love getting up to all kinds of fun together and are always ready for a new scary adventure with the other Rugrats. When these two aren't gobbling worms you'd most probably find them having a good old argument, getting into mischief or making the messiest mud pie you've ever seen! What a pair!

Tommy

Tommy tries his best to make sense of the world through a one-year-old's eyes. It seems a pretty complicated place to be but he leads his gang on adventures to find out about their world and look for answers to all their questions. To him the world is just one giant playground that he intends to explore, swinging his nappy behind him!

MESMERIZING MAZE!

Can you help Tommy find Dil and all his chocolate money?

Answer on page 60

COLOUR ME

Colour in this picture of Susie ice skating!

HE'S SO LOUD, CYNTHIA AND I CAN'T EVEN HEAR OURSELVES THINK!

MEBBE HE'S CRYIN' 'CAUSE HIS DIAPIE IS WET.

WAAAAAAAHHH!

NOPE. ALL DRY!

WAAAAAAHHH!

HUMF! TOO BAD HE'S TOO DUMB TO TELL YOU WHAT HE WANTS.

WE CAN'T MAKE HIM STOP.

WE'VE TRIED EVERYTHING!

I WISH HE COULD TALK. IT WOULD MAKE THINGS EASIER.

YEAH, I'D DO ANYTHING HE'D ASK IF IT WOULD STOP HIS CRYIN'.

ANYTHING DIL ASKS, HUH? HMMMMM.

CYNTHIA AND I ARE GOING INTO THE HOUSE. YOU BALDIES KEEP IT QUIET!

HEY, LISTEN GUYS--DIL STOPPED!

SHHHH! HE FELLED ASLEEP.

THESE BABY MOMITORS SHOULD DO THE TRICK!

SOON...

OKAY, DIL. NOW *YOU'LL* BE ABLE TO ASK CHUCKIE TO DO ANYTHING *I* WANT HIM TO!

HERE HE COMES--THIS IS GONNA BE SOOO GOOD!

I'LL GET IT.

HEY, GUYS, DIL'S AWAKE!

KEEP IT DOWN, CHUCKIE! I'M TRYIN' TO SLEEP LIKE A BABY OVER HERE!

SORRY, DIL, WE DIDN'T MEAN--

HEY! YOU CAN *TALK!*

DIL CAN TALK?

YEAH, IT'S INCREDIBLE! GO AHEAD, DIL. TELL THEM WHAT YOU TOLD ME. GO ON.

POOPY?

HERE YOU GO, DIL. THANKS FOR HELPIN' ME, TOMMY.

THAT'S WHAT BESTEST FRIENDS ARE FOR!

NOW, LET'S GO BEFORE DIL ASKS ME TO GET HIM SOMETHING ELSE!

MINE! MINE!

NO, IT'S MINE! I TOLD CHUCKIE TO GET IT FOR ME, NOT YOU!

ANGELICA! WHAT ARE YOU DOING WITH MY WALKMAN AND THOSE BABY MONITORS?

ANGELICA, THE BABY-TALK 2001 MONITORS ARE NOT TOYS! WAIT UNTIL YOUR FATHER HEARS ABOUT THIS!

BUT, BUT, AUNT DIDI, IT WAS THE BABIES! I DIDN'T DO NOTHIN'!

SO IT WAS ANGELICA TALKING, NOT DIL!

THEN I'M NOT OFF MY ROCKET!

YEAH, IT WAS JUST ANOTHER ONE OF ANGELICA'S MEAN TRICKS!

WELL, THAT PROBLEM IS OVER, BUT I THINK WE GOTS A NEW ONE!

WAAAAAAAAHHHH!

The End

CHUCKIE'S WINTER WORDSEARCH

Can you help Chuckie find these words in the puzzle?

SNOWMAN   SLEDGE   ICICLE

SCARF   HAT   SNOW

SKIS   BOOTS   COAT

GLOVES   COLD   SHIVER

Answers on page 61

```
A E V G S N O W M A N
G B L S H O C E T P Z
J D I C I C L E A P C
G L U U V F S K I S O
L O H C E U T A B U A
O C A O R U S N O W T
V I T B E U U C O L D
E U S C A R F U T U B
S L E D G E H U S F E
```

SPOT THE DIFFERENCE

Can you spot the eight differences between
these two pictures?

Answer on page 60

DOT TO DOT

Can you join the dots to see what Tommy is doing?

Answer on page 61

18

COLOUR ME

Colour in this picture of Angelica!

"Hurry, Chuckie!" Tommy Pickles called out. "Professor Spooky is gonna put a boy into the foocher on TB!"

"Wow," Tommy said. "Wouldn't it be neat to go to the foocher?"

All Growed-Up!

"I don't know, Tommy," said Chuckie. "What if the foocher gots even more scary things than the right-now?"

Tommy patted Chuckie's shoulder. "It wouldn't be scary, Chuckie. 'Cause we'd be biggerer."

"And smarterer," said Kimi.

But Chuckie still looked worried.

Angelica stomped in front of the TV. "This is my new tapiokey machine," she bragged. "I gots a show to do, and you diaper bags are gonna be my applaudience!"

She pressed a button and music began to play.

"Oh, beeyooteeful for spaceship eyes . . . ," Angelica belted out.

"Is it my imagination, or is Angelica getting louderer?" whispered Phil.

"I didn't think Angelica could be louderer," Lil answered.

"For purple mounds of majesty above the fruited rain!" continued Angelica, knocking over everything in sight.

"Hey, Angelica," Tommy said. "Can I try your – "

"NO!" shouted Angelica. "Dumb babies can't play with my stuffs!" And she huffed off.

"It's not fair, you guys," Tommy said with a scowl. "Angelica always plays with our new toys."

"You heard her, Tommy," Chuckie warned. "We're not opposed to play with it."

Tommy picked up the microphone and punched a button. "HELLO?" he said loudly. "Testing, one, two,...LA-LA-LA-LA-LA – "

"HEY!" Angelica shouted. "What do you think you're doing, bald-brain?"

"Ruuuuuuuun!" Chuckie cried.

The babies scattered, dragging the karaoke machine along with them.

Hiding in a cupboard nearby, the babies held on to the doorknob with all their might.

"GIVE ME BACK MY TAPIOKEY MACHINE!" Angelica shrieked as she tugged from the other side.

"What are we going to do?" gasped Chuckie.

"I don't know," Tommy said, "but I'm tired of Angelica bossing us around. She treats us like a bunch of babies!"

"Well, we're not eggsackly growed-ups yet," Chuckie pointed out.

"That's it!" Tommy cried. "We'll go to the foocher! We'll be so growed-up, Angelica won't be able to boss us around."

"But we don't gots a time machine like Professor Spooky," Phil said.

"Sure we do!" Tommy cried. He found an old jump rope in the back of the cupboard and jabbed one end into a deflated basketball. Then he attached the other end to the karaoke machine.

Suddenly the cupboard shook. A bright light flashed.
"Hang on, everybody!" Tommy yelled.
The babies tumbled out of the cupboard . . . and into
the future!

But so did Angelica. "Hand over my new Emica CD!" she shouted.

"But you said we could borrow it," Tommy said. Angelica snatched the CD from Tommy's hand.

"Too bad!"

Ten years older, the gang found themselves in the kitchen eating breakfast. Then Tommy's mum and dad boogied their way in, stopping to strike a pose.

"Oh, Stu, the memories are flooding back!" Didi gushed.

"Uh . . . , Dad, I don't remember you wearing that!"

Dil pointed to the large gold Scorpio medallion hanging from his father's neck.

"Solid gold-plated," Stu said proudly. "I was wearing it the night I met your mum," he added. "It's my good luck charm. I can't dance without it."

"We're going to dance in the Dinosaurs of Disco contest tomorrow night at the park," Didi explained as Stu twirled her around.

As the kids scrambled into the school bus, Angelica hurried to sit with her best friend, Samantha.

"Hey, Angelica, save Chuckie and me a seat!" Tommy shouted. But Angelica looked right past him as if she couldn't see him.

"Check out this cool necklace!" Samantha said. Angelica stared in disbelief. Emica's necklace looked just like her Uncle Stu's Scorpio medallion! "I have the same one," Angelica blurted out. "And I'm gonna wear it to the concert tomorrow night."

"Emica always chooses someone to sing onstage with her," Samantha said. "You're sure to get picked wearing that necklace!"

Chuckie leaned over his seat. He had a strange crumpled look on his face.

"What's wrong?" Tommy asked.

"Samantha almost smiled at me," Chuckie whispered. "I tried to smile back, but my lips got stuck on my new braces." He sighed. "I feel kind of sick – but in a good way."

Wow, Tommy thought. Could Chuckie be . . . in love?

At lunchtime Chuckie saw Samantha again. He patted down his hair.

Chuckie tried to smile, but it looked more like a weird grimace.

"Eww!" Samantha gasped as she hurried past.

"So . . . ," Angelica whispered to Tommy. "Your best friend has a crush on my best friend." She smiled slyly.

"I have a proposition to make. I'll tell Samantha what a great guy Chuckie is – if you get me Uncle Stu's Scorpio necklace. Deal?"

Tommy watched Chuckie dash off to a corner and bury his face in his hands.

"Deal," Tommy groaned.

Tommy knew his dad wouldn't let him borrow the necklace. So he came up with another plan. He'd make a fake. Tommy took some gold foil and wrapped it around a dog biscuit. Then he traced a Scorpio design on top.

"Angelica will get the real one," he told Dil. "Dad will get the fake."

"He'll be really mad if he finds out," Dil warned.

"I know," Tommy said. "But I have to do this for Chuckie!"

Tommy sneaked into his dad's room. He took the real gold necklace and left the fake one in its place. Then he tiptoed out.

Spike awoke with a start. He smelt his favourite treat – Tasty Pooch Snacks. He sniffed high and low, and then he ate the fake necklace in one big gulp!

The next morning Tommy put the real necklace on the kitchen table while he rooted around for his Reptar cereal. Spike spotted the necklace, grabbed it in his mouth, and ran outside.

The garden was littered with bits of gold foil. "Oh, no! Look!" Tommy moaned. "Spike must have eaten the fake necklace and then thought the real one was a dog treat too!"

"How will I dance without my lucky charm?" Stu cried when Tommy told him what had happened.

"Why would you take it without asking?" Didi asked. Angelica had just come in. She shot Tommy a warning look.

"I . . . uh . . . wanted to wear it to the Emica concert so she'd invite me to sing onstage," Tommy fibbed.

"You're grounded," Stu said.

"You'll have to miss the concert," Didi said with a sigh.

"I can't believe you're grounded," Kimi said.

"What a bummer," said Phil as he pulled something out of the sand. "Cool! A Reptar pop!" He popped it into his mouth. "Circa 2001, I'd say."

Just then Spike started digging around in the sandbox. "Hey, what's this?" Lil said, and pulled out –

"My dad's necklace!" Tommy cried. But his parents were already on their way to the dance contest. Tommy and his friends hopped onto their bikes and sped off. Tommy hoped it wasn't too late to get his dad's lucky charm to him. But on the way through the park, Angelica spotted Tommy.

"You found the necklace!" Angelica cried as she lunged for it.

"You can't have it," Tommy said. "If Samantha can't see what a great guy Chuckie is without you telling her, she doesn't deserve him."

"C'mon!" Angelica begged. "Just let me wear it for a minute!"

"Not until you tell the truth," Tommy demanded.

"What's he doing with your necklace?" Samantha asked. Angelica locked eyes with Tommy then she sighed. "He's my cousin," she admitted.

"It's his dad's necklace. He was just gonna let me borrow it."

"Oh, I see," Samantha said. Then she noticed Chuckie. He smiled a great big silver grin. "Don't I know you?" she asked.

"You should!" Angelica blurted. "Samantha Shane, meet Chuckie – I mean, Charles Finster."

Samantha smiled. "Braces were the worst!" she said.
"You know, you're going to be really cute when your
braces come off. Come on. Let's all go sit together."
"Nah, I'll see you guys later," Angelica said.
"What?!" Samantha exclaimed. "And miss Emica?"
Angelica shrugged. "I gotta take care of something."

By the time Tommy, Dil, and Angelica got to the Dinosaurs of Disco contest, Stu and Didi were on the dance floor. Stu was bumping and swivelling in all the wrong places.

"Okay, Dil," Angelica said as she handed him the necklace. "Make this one count!"

Dil threw the necklace toward his dad.

Astonished, Stu caught it – and his rhythm returned. Stu and Didi began to dance like the king and queen of disco!

The kids made it back to the concert just in time for the last song.

"I'm going to need a little help for this next one!" Emica shouted. The spotlight circled the crowd and then stopped on Tommy.

"Pick me too!" Angelica shouted. "Please, please, please! I'm his cousin – and his agent!" They ran up onto the stage together and began to sing with their favourite star.

Angelica grabbed the mike. Tommy tugged back. "It's still my turn!"

"You're forgetting who the star in the family is," Angelica said.

While they wrestled over the mike, a photographer took their picture and – FLASH!

Tommy and his friends tumbled out of the Pickles' cupboard.

"Hey! You broked my tapiokey machine!" Angelica shouted. "You dumb babies better keep your mitts off my stuff for the next bazillion years!"

"Look on the bright side," Tommy told his friends. "Only ten more years till Angelica's nice to us."

SPOT THE DIFFERENCE

Can you spot the six differences between these two pictures?

Answer on page 61

27

28

You have a penalty - THROW AGAIN

30

3

26

Tommy's

You have a penalty - THROW AGAIN

24

23

22

2

Using coins or counters and a dice, be the first to score!

6

START

Spike runs off with the ball - MISS A TURN

1

2

3

4

Football Fun!

| The ball goes over somebody's fence - MISS A TURN | 33 | WINNER |

| 20 | 19 | 18 | 17 |

| You have a penalty - THROW AGAIN | 9 | | 15 |

Feeling thirsty? Stop for a drink - MISS A TURN

| | 10 | | You trip on your laces - GO BACK 2 SPACES |

| 11 | 12 | 13 |

COLOUR ME

Colour in this picture of Chuckie playing baseball!

WHOSE SHADOW?

Can you match up each Rugrat with their shadow?

Answer on page 60

NICE TRY, ANGELICA, BUT YOU'RE NOT GETTING OUT OF EATING YOUR VEGETABLES THAT EASILY.

NOW, AS FOR DIL, HE SEEMS TO BE GOING THROUGH A *HITTING PHASE.* BUT WE'RE GOING TO NIP THIS THING IN THE BUD...

STU, PLEASE KEEP A CLOSE EYE ON DIL WHILE I CONSULT MY LIPSCHITZ LIBRARY. AND MAKE SURE ANGELICA DOESN'T LEAVE THE TABLE UNTIL SHE EATS HER BROCCOLI.

UH... SURE, DEED.

I DON'T UNDERSTAND IT, DEED! THEY'RE KEEPING ALL THE GOOD HITTERS IN THE DUGOUT.

HA! IT LOOKS LIKE SOMEONE SHOULDN'T HAVE BET AGAINST THE HOME TEAM!

WHAT'S GOING ON, TOMMY?

I DON'T KNOW, CHUCKIE. I THINK DIL IS IN TROUBLE WITH MY MOMMY...

HE'S IN TROUBLE, ALL RIGHT! DIL'S ABOUT TO GET SENT TO THE *BUGHOUSE!*

THE BUG-HOUSE?

I WANNA GO, TOO! I WAS GETTING KIND OF HUNGRY.

HOW 'BOUT SOME BROCCOLI?

UH...NO THANKS. I'D RATHER SAVE MY APPETITE FOR THE BUG-HOUSE.

YOU DON'T WANNA GO *THERE*, YOU DUMB BABY. IT'S A BORING PLACE WHERE YOU SIT AROUND ALL DAY AND SPIT WHILE EVERYONE ELSE GETS TO PLAY.

HA, HA! YOUR TEAM DOESN'T STAND A CHANCE AGAINST OUR PITCHER!

THREE STRIKES, YOU'RE OUT, AND IT'S BACK TO THE DUGOUT! HEH-HEH.

DID YOU HEAR WHAT GRANDPA SAID? THREE STRIKES AND YOU'RE OUT OF HERE!

DIL ALREADY TOOK TWO SWINGS AT ME. ONE MORE AND THEY'RE GONNA SEND HIM TO THE BUGHOUSE JUST LIKE I SAID.

THAT'S NOT TRUE, IS IT, TOMMY? DIL WON'T BE ALLOWED TO PLAY WITH US ANYMORE?

YOU WOULDN'T TELL ON A POOR IN-A-CENT BABY, WOULD YOU, ANGELICA?

IN-A-CENT?

DID YOU SEE HOW HE TRIED TO *HIT* ME WITH HIS ICKY DROOLY HANDS?

MAYBE HE JUST WANTED TO PLAY "TICKLES," ANGELICA.

OR "PATTY CAKE." I DON'T LIKE PLAYING "TICKLES."

YUCKIE...?

HMPH! IF IT'S NOT ICKY VEGETABLES, IT'S DUMB BABIES HITTING ME.

THIS IS WHAT I HAVE TO DEAL WITH AROUND HERE...

WHAT ARE WE GONNA *DO*, TOMMY? I DON'T WANT DIL TO GO TO NO BUG-HOUSE.

I DON'T NEITHER, CHUCKIE!

WE HAVE TO WATCH DIL WITH A CLOSED EYE.

BUT IF MY EYES ARE CLOSDED, HOW CAN I *WATCH* HIM?

AND HOW DO WE KNOW WHEN HE WANTS TO HIT ANGELICA?

UM...I THINK WE'LL SEE HIS "HITTING FACE," LIKE MY MOMMY SAID.

WHAT'S A "HITTING FACE," ANYWAY?

MAYBE IT'S THE LOOK HE HAS ON HIS *FACE* WHEN HE WANTS TO *HIT* SOMEONE!

YOU MEAN LIKE *THAT!?*

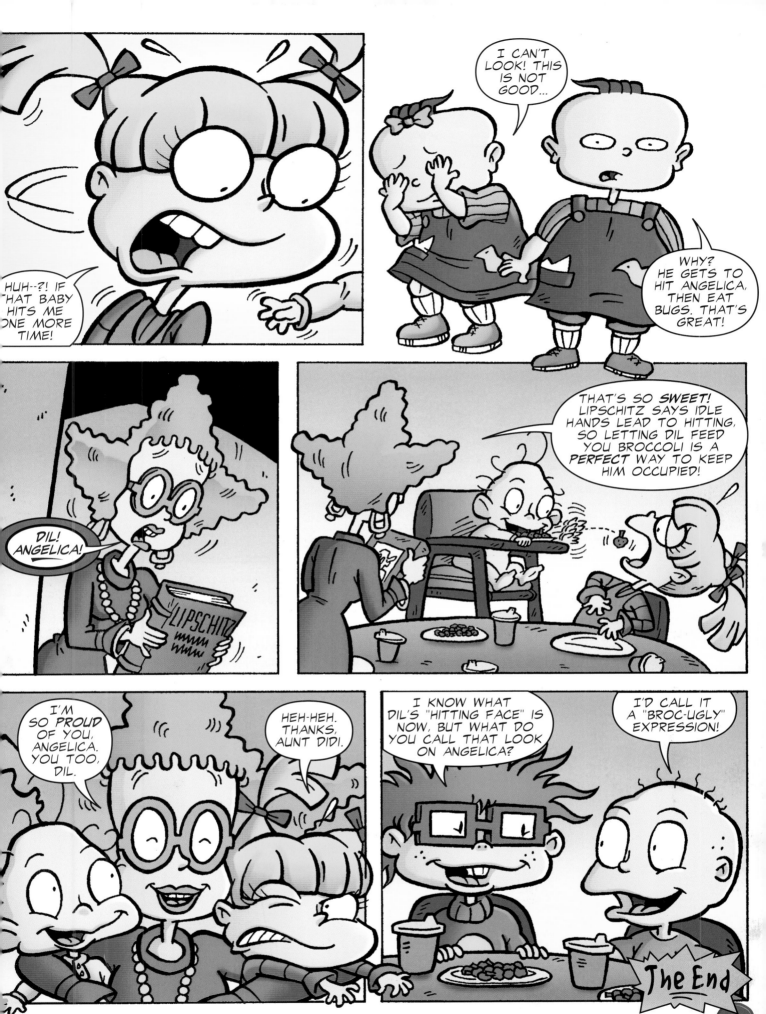

ANSWERS

WHOSE SHADOW?

Can you match up each Rugrat with their shadow?

SPOT THE DIFFERENCE

Can you spot the eight differences between these two pictures?

MESMERIZING MAZE!

Can you help Tommy find Dil and all his chocolate money?

60

CHUCKIE'S! WINTER WORDSEARCH

Can you help Chuckie find these words in the puzzle?

SNOWMAN   SLEDGE   ICICLE
SCARF   HAT   SNOW
SKIS   BOOTS   COAT
GLOVES   COLD   SHIVER

```
A E V G S N O W M A N
G B L S H O C E T P Z
J D I C C L E A P C
G L U U V F S K I S O
L O H C E U T A B U A
O C A O R U S N O W T
V I T B E U U C O L D
E U S C A R F U T U B
S L E D G E H U S F E
```

DOT TO DOT

Can you join the dots to see what Tommy is doing?

SPOT THE DIFFERENCE

Can you spot the six differences between these two pictures?